The Grandson
of a
Sharecropper

Eddie Gaston Jr.

ISBN 979-8-89428-859-8 (paperback)
ISBN 979-8-89428-860-4 (digital)

Christian Faith Publishing
832 Park Avenue
Meadville, PA 16335
www.christianfaithpublishing.com

Printed in the United States of America

The year is 1945, World War II had just ended, but the activities of war were still in full swing. Warplanes flew about; soldiers played war games in the wooded areas. It appeared that everything was on high alert. The United States of America had dropped bombs on two cities in Japan. That, along with the invasion of Normandy, ended the war.

It was a Sunday morning; a lot was happening in the county of Fairfield South Carolina. This month, the second Sunday in August, was an exciting and momentous day in the Mount Zion AME Church, member's life. It was Mount Zion's turn to host the "big meeting." Fairfield County was a mule-farming county. The main money crops were cotton and corn, and the farmers planted other crops for food such as peanuts, field peas, potatoes, and sugar cane.

Sometime around the early 1900, a group of Black churches in Fairfield County, South Carolina, met together and formed a union. It was voted on, and then an agreement was made that on a given Sunday in the year, a church was to host the meeting; it was agreed that each church would be given one week during the summer to host the big meeting. All the churches in the association were very diligent about keeping the Sunday they were assigned. Different guest church choirs were assigned to pervade the music for the week; there would be as many as three guest church choirs that were selected to sing each night. Each church service started on Sunday and ended the following Friday night.

This coming Sunday was the beginning of a series of big meetings. The big meeting was not only for great singing and preaching but also it was the big social event of the year. The entire county gathered to worship, eat, socialize with each other, and have fun. There was always the opportune time to find a husband or a wife.

Piney Grove Baptist Church was hosting the first big meeting of the series. The Jeter family were members of the Mount Zion AME church a few miles away; Rosa could not wait for Sunday evening to come. She had her eyes on a handsome young man with a deep gravel voice who was the bass singer in the Piney Grove Baptist Church choir. They had talked briefly once before, and Rosa liked him, and she believed that he liked her. She was thinking about him all week, praying that she did not miss the opportunity to talk to him this Sunday at Pine Grove Church.

That week, Rosa was busy doing things around the house without being told; she even volunteered to cook dinner. Alice, Rosa's mother, was observing her oldest daughter and wondered why she was so willing and appeared to be looking for something to do this week without being told to do so. Rosa had never been that energetic in her short life.

As Rose was going back and forth in the house doing whatever she could find to keep herself busy, Alice could not help but notice her oldest daughter and her uncommon helpfulness and her unusual activities and wondered what she was up to. Alice could not wait any longer.

She called out, "Sis, come here."

Sis was Rosa's nickname, which was short for sister.

When Rosa heard the sharp and demanding voice of her mother, she quickly stopped and answered, "Yes, Mom."

Alice replied, "What do you want? You are not doing all this work without being told for nothing, so what is it?"

"Nothing, Ma," Rosa replied with her head down.

"Quit lying. What is it?" asked her mother.

With her head still down looking at the floor, Rosa replied in a soft voice, "Well, Ma, you know that the Pine Grove Church's big meeting is this coming Sunday, and I was wondering if you could make me a dress for the meeting."

Her mother stopped what she was doing and looked at her oldest daughter for what seemed like a long time and realized that her oldest daughter was becoming a young woman and interested in boys.

Alice lowered her head for a few seconds as if in deep, soul-searching thought.

After a minute or two, she slowly raised her head and said, "Well, you all worked hard in the field this year, and we are very proud of you. All of you did exceptionally well, and because of the hard work you all put in the farm, we made a good crop of cotton. The corn did very well. Also, and I don't think I heard any of you complain once. I will talk to your dad and see what I can do.

Alice wasted no time; she went out on the front porch where David, her husband, was sitting in his favorite old rocking chair; he was watching the birds of many types and colors as they played and feasted on what they found in the yard and listening to the squeaking of the chair as he slowly rocked back and forth and chewed on a very short cigar. Alice walked over to where David was sitting. She sat in the chair next to him and began to rock very slowly; she was listening to the sequencing of the loose boards under the chair as it rocked back and forth as she was searching for the right words to say.

Then choosing her words very carefully, not looking at David, she said, "David, you know we have some real wonderful children; they made me so proud of them this year. Those children worked hard in the field this year, and we did better than alright for a change. I thank the cotton crop did better than we expected it to; it turned out to be a very good crop, and it did very well. Even though Mr. Thursday took most of the money but overall, we did alright.

David moved that old very short cigar from one side of his mouth to the other with only his tongue and lips and spit off the porch.

He then moved the cigar back to where it was and said in a very matter-of-fact tone, "What do you want now, Alice. I can tell by the tone of your voice that you want something." Looking up to the sky as if he was thinking, David went on and said, "Let me see now... last year, I got you a living room set so the girls will have a place to keep company. The year before that, I got you a new cookstove so that the house won't get all smoked up every time you lit a fire in it. Now what is it that you want now?"

Alice selected her words very carefully and said, "I don't want anything for myself. But those girls worked hard this year, and I am very proud of them. I was wondering if we could spend a few dollars to get them some dresses. I will make the dresses. I just need a few dollars to buy the clothes to make them. They need some new dresses."

David took the cigar out of his mouth and spit out of the same side the cager was in.

He then turned and looked at Alice, but before he could say anything, Alice babbled and said, "I would make the dresses, all I need is the cloth."

"How much money will you need?" David asked as he began to chew on the short cigar.

"About $11 ought to be enough," Alice replied.

David began a slow rocking back and forth looking at the little bird as they played in the new growth of gross in the front yard, and said, "Are you making dresses for all the girls?"

Alice said, "Yes, I cannot make dresses for one and not the others."

After a bit of hesitation as if he was in deep thought, David said, "Alright, go ahead."

Alice wasted no time; she knew that time was short if she was going to have those dresses ready for the big meeting, she needed to hurry. She made her way into the bedroom; after a quiet glance around the room, she raised the bed mattress on one side and retrieved a small black bag from its hiding place. It was tied at one end with a small string. Alice untied the rope and reached inside. After recovering the money from its place of safety, she put the bag back under the mattress and returned to the porch.

Willie, Alice, and David's oldest child were playing a game called Jack Rocks at the far end of the porch with his little brother David Junior.

Alice called his name, "Willie, Come here."

Willie heard his mother call his name, "Willie, come here."

He was so involved in the game that he did not attend to his mother's call.

Then he was shaken by a very demanding voice saying, "Willie, did you hear me," I said come here, and I mean right now.

As if the small rock he was holding in his hand was a very hot potato, Willie quietly dropped the rock and went to his mother and said, "Yes, Ma."

Willie was a seventeen-year-old young man—tall and slim and stood at just a little over six feet. When he heard his mother's voice, he readily left the jack rock game and went to her.

He said, "Yes, Mom."

His mother, holding the $12 in her hand, said, "I want you to go over to Mrs. Lighter's house. Tell her that I would like to get seven feed sacks, but I would like them all a different color if she has them. Don't pay her until she tells you how much it is, and you come straight home. I want to start on your sisters' dresses as soon as possible."

Willie said, "Yes, Mom," and off he went.

Willie was glad to get out of the eyesight of his mother so he could have a smoke on a short cigarette.

Mrs. Lighter lived about one mile away. She was a middle-aged White lady who *raised chickens and sold the eggs. The feed for the chickens came in large sacks.* The feed sacks were constructed from good cloth that was beautiful and colorful. They had many different patterns, shapes, and colors. The grain company made the feed sacks out of good cloth, and the cloth was easy to look at, and the bags were big enough so that the customer would buy the feed so that they could sell the sacks to the impoverished local folk who didn't have enough money to buy store-bought clothes.

The next few days, after farmwork was done and house chores completed, it was bustling in the Jeter's house. Alice was busy fitting, cutting, and sewing. All the while, there was a big half-hidden smile on her face as she was cutting and sowing; she was known as a very good sentry, and people would come from all over the neighborhood and ask her to make dresses for them. But for Alice, making the dresses for her daughters was a labor of pure love, and she loved every minute of it. The singer-sewing machine lived up to its name; it sang a sweet tune as Alice put pressure on the plate.

It was the first Sunday in June; the Jeter family had returned from Mount Zion AME Church where the Jesters are faithful members. David was an officer in the church. Alice sang in the church choir. Rosa and Annabelle, Alice and David's two oldest daughters, helped their mother fix Sunday dinner. David had killed one of the fatted yard chickens, and they were having buttermilk cornbread, fried chicken, rice, and collard greens with a big picture of grape Kool-Aid made with fresh spring water to wash it all down. Alice opened a jar of peaches she had canned last summer and made a very delicious peach pie for dessert.

After a delicious and well-cooked dinner, David went out on the front porch, took a set in his favorite rocking chair, took out his pipe and a can of Prince Albert smoking tobacco out of his pocket. He very carefully poured a small amount of tobacco into the pipe, packed it in with his index finger and lit the pipe with a long match. After taking a few puffs of the pipe, he leaned back in his chair as if he was announcing the end of today's activities and had a long satisfying smoke; why listen to the *Amos n' Andy* show on an old battery-powered radio? The radio had a battery that was larger than the radio itself. There was a long wire that ran overhead, from the house to a tall pole about thirty feet away from the side of the house which served as the radio antenna.

They had no electrical service and no running water. They had to walk a mile to get drinking water from a hole in the ground. As David and Alice sat on the front porch, David Junior walked by, and Alice asked Junior whose turn it was to get water for the night.

"I thank it is my turn, Ma," David Junior replied.

"Well, what are you waiting for? Go get the water before it gets too dark, you know the snakes are crawling, and look where you put your feet."

As David Junior left to get the water, David Senior said, "You know it would be nice to have a water wall right in the backyard like White folks."

Alice said, "David, that seems like a good idea to me. What's wrong with that? I think we can do it."

After talking it over with the family, they made plans to dig the well, and they selected a good spot a few feet from the house. All the male members of the family took turns digging; the females provided the food, and everyone was excited over the possibility of having water right in the backyard and not having to carry water a mile. They made the plan, and the well-digging began. Every male member of the Jeter house took part in the well-digging, but their dream was short-lived; the landowner, Mr. Thursday, found out that the Jesters were digging a water well right in the backyard.

Late one evening, just after the evening sun went down, the Jeter family was relaxing on the front porch when they heard the sound of a pickup truck coming down the driveway at a high speed; the driver put on his breaks and slid up to the porch with dust flying everywhere. It was Mr. Thursday; after stopping the truck, he poked his head out the window.

Without greeting the Jeter family or allowing them to greet him, he leaned his head out of the truck window and said, "I hear that you people are digging a well on my land. I want you to stop it, and I mean right now. What do you think you are? White folks? Well, you are not White folks. You are just nuggets, and you need to stay in your place. Stop digging and get your water from the hole in the ground like you always did, you hear what I say. I don't know what's getting into Black people these days, they always want to be something they are not. You are not White, you are just black folks who are working my land, so stay in your place."

David said, "Yes, sir. Mr. Thursday, we are stopping right now."

With that, Mr. Thursday quietly drove off at the same speed he came in with and said, "There will be no water well digging here. Get your water from the hole in the ground down the hill like you always did."

Mr. Thursday left nothing but dust. David Junior looked at his father and asked Daddy why Mr. Thursday didn't want them to have a well.

David Senior looked at his son for a minute and said, "Well, son, it is like this, most White folks—not all, mind you, but most of them—don't think colored folks should have the nice things that White folks have. They think that we should not have water right in the house as White folks do. They think we should not have a nice white painted house like they do. That is why our house is painted black, but don't worry about it; another day is coming, and it won't be very long.

Then David Junior looked at his father with a puzzled look on his face and said, "What do you mean, Daddy?"

His daddy replied, "Just keep on living, son, just keep on living, and you will find out one day, and it won't be very long. The day is coming when your children and my grands will drive fine automobiles and live in beautiful houses—all clean and white and trimmed in green, the color of grass after a nice spring rain, with fresh clean water running in the kitchen and bright shine electric lights. You don't have to worry about oil in your lamp. The only oil you will need is the oil of Jesus, Mary's baby boy, running in your veins. We need some oil in our lamps—the oil that makes us love those that despitefully use us and abuse us. It is the oil that the woman with the issue of blood had when she touched the hem of Jesus garment and she was made whole again—the same oil that blind Bartimaeus had when he called on the name of Jesus and received his sight. It is that same oil that makes us love our enemies—that Holy Ghost oil that has our lamp of love trimmed and shining a bright beam of love on those that hate us and use us and abuse us. Let us have the love of the Lord Jesus in our heart that we may have peace." Then David began to sing a tone: "By and by, when the morning comes, when all the saints are joined together as one. We will tell the story of how we overcome, we will understand it better by and by..."

Then everyone joined in and began to sing. The singing eased the saddest that was in everyone's heart.

*****

Rosa woke up early the following morning so that she could try on her new dress. Her mother was sitting at the sewing machine.

Rosa broke the silence and said, "Ma, is the dress finished yet?"

"Yes, it's finished," the mother replied. "Go on, and try it on."

Like a little child with a new toy, Rosa grabbed the dress, went into the next room, and put the dress on. She came back out and stood in front of the mirror. There was a unique mirror that allowed the person standing in front of it to see themselves from all angles. The mirror had three parts: one part was stationary and could not be moved. The two-sided mirror was on hinges and could move so that the person in front of it could see themselves front and back and both sides depending on the position of the two-side mirror.

Rosa stood in front of the mirror, turning every way she could to make sure the dress fitted the way she wanted. The trimerous smile on her face that said this is it let you know that she was well-pleased with what she saw. Rosa's sisters, Annabelle and Clementine, walked into the room and observed Rosa admiring herself in the mirror.

Annabelle commented and said, "Look, there she is, trying to make herself look good for that old Eddie Gaston."

Rosa turned and looked at them with a sarcastic smile and said, "I am not trying. I am doing it. And as far as that old Eddie Gaston, as you call him, is concerned, this dress and the fine-looking thing that is wearing it will put a hook in his mouth. I think that is enough now."

"Rosa, don't wear that dress out before Sunday gets here."

The other sisters Annabelle, Clementine, Dazelle, and Thelma all took their turn in front of the mirror, looking and turning this way and that way to make sure that their clothing was suitable and fitted the way they wanted. All the girls seemed to be happy with their dress, and that made Alice more than happy.

*****

It was Saturday morning. The Jeter household was busy preparing for the Sunday morning worship at the Mount Zion AME Church. They had a busy Sunday fast approaching. After church at

Mt Zion, the family will be headed for Pine Grove to participate in their big meeting. Rosa was up early, making sure she had everything in place. Rosa was very excited, not about attending church at Mount Zion. But if she wanted to get to Pine Grove, she had to go to Mount Zion first because her parents were not coming back home after attending services at Mount Zion. They were going straight to Pine Grove so they could be there for the start of their big meeting: the evening service.

*****

That Sunday morning, all the Jeter girls, with Alice and David, packed into the family's 1926 A-model Ford. And off they went to morning worship at Mount Zion AME Church. They rolled up on the church ground simultaneously with brother Oscar Cook—the church choir master. Old man John Cook and Alice's father and mother had just pulled up in his two-seated buggy pulled by a high-stepping jet-black horse. Brother John Cook had taught the horse to dance in place at his command, so they put on a little show. As the high-stepping horse came dancing onto the church ground, Mrs. Claria Cook, his wife, was sitting in the front seat right beside her husband with her Sunday go-to-meeting bonnet tied under her chin nice and secure. The couple was the mother and father of Alice, and her sister, Hattie Mae, was in the back seat with two of her daughters. The only brother Alice had died at a very young age.

Before David could park the car, Mr. Joe Brown pulled up to the church ground from a side road and parked his wagon pulled by a well-fed work mule. His sons and daughters had come to worship with him and his wife. The worshippers kept coming until the churchyard was full. Some came walking, and some came riding. But they all came dressed up in their best Sunday's go-to-meeting. It was not quite time for the worship service to begin. The womenfolk went inside the church and sat in their favorite seat, waiting for the devotion service. David was the devotion leader this Sunday. He pulled his pocket watch from his watch pocket to check the time, looking at the other men as if to say, let us go in and start. David began to walk toward the front door of the church, the other men right behind him. The men went inside the church and took a seat.

Brother Joe Brown picked up a small table and set it in front of the congregation. David and brother Joe Brown stood behind the wooden table. David picked up a hymn book and began to line the hymn, "What a friend we have in Jesus, all our sins and griefs to bear. What a privilege it is to carry everything to God in prayer." Before he could finish the first line, Brother Oscar Cook, the choirmaster, began to sing, and the church followed. The church had no musical instrument; they had only their hands and feet to make music. However, just a few seconds into the hymn, feet started patting hitting the floor in perfect rhythm with the hymn; the entire wooden floor of the church became a giant drum, and it was indeed good music. After the singing of the melody, brother Joe leads the church in prayer, and what a powerful prayer he prayed. He prayed for everybody and their brothers, and a few other folks turned in.

After the prayer, Sister Boyd stood up and began to sing the song, "Call Him by his name just call him Jesus." Some folks were standing on their feet clapping and waving their hand in agreement. Sister Boyd would sing another verse:

> When you are in trouble
> Just call him
> Call him by his name
> Call him by his name
> When you are sick, call him by his name
> Call him by his name
> When you in trouble, call him by his name
> Call him by his name!
> Just call him Jesus O Lord Jesus, O Lord Jesus
> You just call him by his name

The preacher got up and preached a short sermon afterward; he extended the invite to Christian discipleship. Brother Oscar Cook and his choir put on a mini concert while the officers were taking up the collection. After this, the preacher reminded everyone that the church members had an obligation to be at the Pine Grove Baptist Church for their big meeting beginning today at three o'clock. Brother Cook reminded them that they needed to be on time because they had to sing.

After church, the members left in a hurry getting in mule-drawn wagons and horse-drawn carriages. Some were getting in their cars and trucks. Those who did not have some other forms of transportation were getting rides any way they could. They just wanted to go in the direction of the big meeting.

Rosa and her family were on their way to the Pine Grove's big meeting. Rosa was sure that she would get to see that fantastic figure of a man with the deep voice once again. Down the road, they went in the black 1926 Model T Ford.

Finally, they made it to the Pine Grove Church. Cars, trucks, and horse-drawn wagon buggies were everywhere. It was not easy for David to find a place to park; after finally finding a parking spot, they got out of the vehicle and began to make their way to the front of the church. The singing coming from the church filled their ears as they hurried to get inside to take part in and enjoy the excellent singing coming from the inside; it sounded like they were having a shouting good time in there. Everyone began to move a little faster as they made their way to the front door because they did not want to miss anything. They wanted to be in on that singing and shouting. Pine Grove choir began to sing. They were one of the best choirs in the union.

Even though they were about six rows of benches apart, yet Rosa and Eddie's eyes found each other. Eddie's singing was getting louder and louder; it was as if he were singing only for and to Rosa. Out of all the singing, Rosa exclusively heard him. For Eddie and Rosa, cupid was in the building, and it was flying around on the wings of love and landed on both; love was in the air.

After the worship service was over, everyone went outside for the feast. All the Pine Grove members had brought baskets of food so that they could feed the guests. The members of Pine Grove were busy preparing and serving food for all that wanted it. And that meant everyone. It looked like every car and trunk and in the back of each wagon, a food box was open. They were preparing to serve those who had come to worship with them. The people came, and a great feast was on.

Rosa and Eddie found a quiet spot so that they could talk.

Eddie asked, "Are you keeping company with anyone?"

"Why did you ask that?" replied Rosa.

Eddie said, "I would like to come to see you on Sundays after church if that's alright."

Rosa looked him in the eye, trying to hide her excitement, and said, "You will have to ask my daddy."

"Do I have to ask Mr. Son Jeter? Can I just ask your mom?"

"No," Rosa replied, "you must ask my dad."

Eddie found the courage to ask Mr. Son Jeter if he could keep company with his oldest daughter. David looked Eddie up and down, then he rolled that old cigar but to the other side of his mouth and spit then rolled the cigar back to where it was.

"You are sister Nora Mobile, boy, are you?"

Eddie said, "Miss Mobile raised me since I was a baby after my mother died."

"I see," David replied with his eyes still on Eddie. "Who is your daddy?" David asked.

"My dad's name is Josh Gaston."

"And where is your dad and mama?"

Eddie replied, "They were not here, they separated when I was a baby. His name was Josh Gaston."

"Where is he now," David asked. "And where is your mother?"

Eddie's face began to fill with anger, then he said in a very hash tone looking Mr. Jeter in the eye, Eddie said, "Mr. Jeter, my daddy cut off my mother's foot with an axe, and she died, and my daddy left town, and I have not seen him since. Is that what you want to know?" But Eddie wouldn't be put. "Mr. Jeter, can I keep company with your daughter or not, Sir?"

David replied, "Sure, you can, son," without stopping or looking in Eddie's direction.

Eddie replied, "Thank you, Sir. I thank you." Eddie went to Rosa and said, "Guess what?"

"I don't want to guess," said Rosa. "What did Daddy say?"

"He said I could come to see you," replied Eddie.

Rosa was filled with excitement, but she did not want Eddie to know it.

"I will see you Sunday," Rosa said.

"What time shall I be there?" Eddie asked.

"Any time after supper," said Rosa.

All the next week, Rosa was looking at the calendar wishing that Sunday would be a little sooner.

*****

Sunday finally came. Eddie came home from Pine Grove Church to eat some of what Miss Nora had cooked. He changed his shirt, dusted the dust off his shoes, and started on the four-mile walk to Rosa's house.

On the way, Eddie was wondering how he would greet Rosa's mother, but Mr. Son Jeter was another story.

Eddie had to do a little walking to get to Rosa's house; after walking about four miles, he turned off onto a small footpath. It was a warm summer evening with a cool breeze blowing in the treetops. It appeared that everything in the woods was preparing for spring and building a nest to raise their young. As he walked looking up into the treetops, he observed the squirrels jumping from limb to limb, building a home for their young. Spring was in the air; everything was looking for a mate, and so was he.

Eddie followed the winding footpath. It led him right to Rosa's front porch. Rosa's mother and father were sitting on the front porch. He greeted them, and Rosa's father told him that Rosa was in the living room, and he could go on in. But by then, Rosa was at the door.

She pulled the door open a little further and said, "Come in."

When Eddie walked in, Rosa's other four sisters left the room, just like Rosa had planned it.

They sat there in the living room and got to know each other. Rosa felt like she knew him, and he felt like he knew her. The first visit went well; Rosa was happy and at peace all week and could hardly wait for next Sunday.

Rosa was now seventeen years old and had fondly found someone that she wanted to be with. It appeared that the family liked him too. He even got along with her brothers.

The week went by fast; before you knew it, Sunday was here again, and a five-foot-nine figure of a young man with a steady gait came with his head high like he was the gift to the world walking down the footpath on his way to see his waiting sweetheart. This would be the third time in as many weeks that he was at Rosa's house.

He kept walking down the path; as he walked, he observed the birds making their nest. The squirrels were busy jumping from limb to limb as they built their nest. As he walked, a black shack crossed his path. But he paid little mind. His mind was on Rosa. Eddie reached into his shirt pocket and pulled out a pack of Lucky Strike cigarettes. He took a box of matches out of his pants' pocket and lit it up. He took a long drag on that Lucky Strike and let the smoky ease from his mouth a little at a time. The smoke disappeared into the air behind him as he walked.

Eddie was letting the drifting smoke fly and drift into the evening air as if he did not have a single care in the world. It was just him, the green trees, the winding footpath, and the small animals running all around him, and the thought of Rosa was the only thing on his mind. At the top of the hill that was filled with new undergrowth, he heard someone say, there comes Eddie. At the sound of the voice, Eddie squared up his shoulders, lifted his head, and went stepping up to the house like he was the gift of life. This was his fourth Sunday that he had walked the beaten path that was impregnated with wildlife and beautiful undergrowth that led to Rosa's house; he was beginning to be at ease. Everyone was very nice to him, he and Rosa's brother Willie hit it off from the start, but as for Mr. Jeter, he was still trying to figure him out.

Eddie and Rosa had a seat in the living room. The sound of constant cow bellowing filled the air and appeared to make all other sounds disappear. To the Jeter family, it was a sound that said I need milking.

Alice's voice rang out, "Whose turn is it to milk the cow?"

"It is Sis's turn, Ma," said Annabelle.

Rosa tried to get one of her sisters to take her turn but had no luck; she had no takers.

Rosa said, "Annabelle, would you milk the cow for me today? I will milk for you next time."

Annabelle said, "Sorry, Sis, but it is your turn to milk the cow."

No one would milk the cow for Rosa. She pleaded with her sisters, but no one would come to her aid.

Eddie said, "Come on, I will go with you."

Rosa grabbed the milk pail and headed for the barn. The barn was about seventy-five yards away from the house. It was between the house and the milking rack. Mr. Jeter had to build a milking rack to keep the cow from kicking over the milk pail.

Once Eddie and Rosa lost sight of the house, there was a lot of playing, hugging, and kissing taking place, so much so that they lost track of time. The cow started bellowing again. The sharp voice of Rosa's mother rang out.

"Rosa, you have not milked that cow yet. What are you doing out there?"

"We are milking the cow, Ma. I will be finished in a minute."

Rosa had never, in her short life, milked a cow that fast. In a few minutes, Rosa and Eddie came from around the barn; Eddie carried the milk pail, and Rosa walked beside him.

*****

A little more than a month had passed since Eddie and Rosa encountered cow milking. Early one Saturday morning, Rosa took some leftover table scraps out to the chicken pen. When it appeared for no reason at all, Rosa began to feel sick. She started to throw up. All her breakfast was lying in a messy heap on the ground. Rosa was on her knees, looking down at the mass.

Then the voice of Clementine rang out calling their mother.

"Ma, come out here for a minute."

The sound of Clementine's voice made Alice move fast. She knew that something was wrong. Alice ran down the back porch and made her way to the corner of the house where Rosa was still on her knees, looking very sick.

Alice put her hand on her daughter's back and said, "What is the matter?"

"I don't know, Ma. The same thing happened yesterday morning and the morning before that."

Alice slowly pulled her hand from her daughter's back and stood slanted for a few minutes, then she asked Rosa a question, "Did you have your monthly period last month?"

Rasa, sounding like she was about to cry, said, "No, Ma."

Alice's face appeared to take on another shape then she asked Rosa another question, "Have you had your period this month yet?"

Rosa, with tears falling from her chin, said in a very soft voice, "No, Ma."

Then Alice, in a loud tone of voice, said, "Get up from there, your fast-tail is pregnant. It is that old Eddie Gaston with his no-good self. I knew he was up to something he was not going down to that barn every Sunday for nothing. Get up from there and go into the house!"

*****

Well, Sunday evening was here again. And just as it has happened Sunday after Sunday, just before the evening sun goes down, the five-foot-ten-inch figure of a young man came walking through the footpath smoking on a Lucky Strike and blowing smoke as he walked with a steady gait.

Mr. Jeter and his wife, Alice, were sitting on the porch in the rocking chairs.

Eddie walked up to the porch and said, "Good evening."

No one said a word. The silence made Eddie feel very uneasy. As usual, Willie and his brother David Junior were on the other end of the porch playing a game.

Willie said, "Rosa is inside, go on in."

Eddie had a very unpleasant feeling that made him think that something was wrong. It made him feel very unwelcome. But he pulled the screen door open and walked in. Eddie found Rosa sitting on a chair with her eyes red from crying.

"What's wrong, Rosa?" he asked.

Rosa started crying all over again.

Eddie asked, "Are you sick?"

"No," Rosa replied.

"Then what is wrong?" Eddie kept on questioning Rosa, trying to find out why she was crying.

Then without warning, Rosa yelled out, "I am pregnant" as if she was blaming Eddie; she looked at Eddie as if she was angry at him.

Eddie looked at her for a long time then sat down beside her, put his arm around her waist, and said, "You know I love you, I was trying to get up the nerves to ask you to marry me. Now is as good a time as any."

Rosa said, "I don't want you to marry me just because I am with child. If that is the reason, I don't want to marry you."

Eddie said, "Rosa, you are the best woman that ever put on a pair of shoes and slipped a frock over your head. I will marry you with a child or without a child."

Rosa walked off a few paces, and Eddie followed her.

Eddie grabbed her by the hand and said, "Well, what do you say?"

"Yes," answered Rosa, "but you will have to ask my daddy."

Eddie was unsure if he wanted to talk to Mr. Son Jeter right now, but he made his way around to the slightly sloping front porch where Mr. Jeter was. He was there sitting in an old rocking chair, rocking slowly as usual when he had something on his mind, looking at the birds playing in the yard.

Eddie greeted Mr. Jeter, and without looking him in the eye, he said, "Mr. Jeter, can I talk to you a minute?"

Just as always, Mr. Jeter rolled that cigar but to the other side of his mouth and spit.

He looked at Eddie and said, "I am listening."

"Well," Eddie said, trying to find the right words to say, "I want to know, Sir, if I can have your permission to marry your daughter."

As if he didn't know, Mr. Jeter asked, "Which daughter do you wish to marry?"

Eddie looked at him with a puzzled look on his face and replied, "Rosa, Sir," Eddie answered in a way that meant who else?

Mr. Jeter said, "Why do you want to marry Rosa?"

Eddie replied, "Well—"

Before Eddie could say another word, Mr. Jeter said, "Do you have a job?"

Eddie replied, "No, sir."

"Do you have any money?"

"I have $4, sir."

Mr. Jeter looked Eddie in the eye and said in a sorry kind of way, "Four whole dollars, well, and you don't have a job?" Mr. Jeter asked.

Eddie said, "No, sir."

"Well, young man, the country is in a depression right now. Everybody and his brother are looking for a job. What makes you think you can find one?"

"I will find something," Eddie replied.

Mr. Jeter sat back and started looking at the birds as they flew back and forth, putting grass and whatever they could find into the birdhouses that Mr. Jeter had built. Mr. Jeter continued watching the birds go in and out of the birdhouses building their nest. Eddie was becoming impatient. Mr. Jeter had not given him an answer to his question.

Eddie, speaking in a different tone of voice, and looking Mr. Jeter, right in the eye, said, "Mr. Jeter, could Rosa and I get married or not?"

Mr. Jeter took the cigar out of his mouth, looked for a minute or two, and then he asked, "Do you have any money, son?"

"Yes, sir, I have $4, sir."

Mr. Jeter looked at Eddie and said, "You don't say four whole dollars." He said it again very slowly, "You have four whole dollars and you want to get married."

"Well, sir—"

Mr. Jeter said, "Well, son, I tell you what, you seem to be very bullheaded about getting married. You give me three of those dollars, and you can have my blessing, and I am expecting you to take excellent care of my daughter. If that is clear, you can marry her."

With some hesitation, Eddie took out of his pocket $3. Mr. Jeter took the $3 and, without looking at them, put them in his shirt pocket and continued to observe the *birds as they played in the yard.*

*****

The following Saturday, Mr. Jeter, his wife, Alice, Rosa, and Eddie jumped into Mr. Jeter's Model T Ford and headed for the town of Winnsboro so that Eddie and Rosa could get married by the justice of the peace. The ceremony was very short. Rosa was wearing the dress that her mother had made for her. Eddie was wearing a pair of blue pants and his good shirt. They both said I do. Rosa signed her name. Eddie made his X, and someone else signed his name for him because he could not read or write. Eddie paid for the wedding with money he had borrowed.

On the way back home, everyone was hushed. Alice broke the silence. Where are you two planning to live, as if to say there is no room for you at our house. Everyone was silent.

Looking back at Eddie, Mr. Jeter said, "Do you have any place for your wife to live, son?"

Rosa looked at Eddie with a look of wonder on her face.

Eddie spoke and said, "We would live with my aunt until we got a place of our own."

After that was settled, no one spoke. All you could hear was the put-put of the Model T Ford motor as they zipped down the road at forty miles per hour.

They arrived home, and Rosa's sisters and brothers greeted them. They all welcomed Eddie into the family. Rosa and her four sisters went into the back room for some girls' talk while Rosa packed her clothes to move to her new home. Eddie and Willie went around to the side of the house. They wanted to get out of sight of Alice so they could smoke a cigarette.

When Rosa was packed and ready to move to her new home, they all said goodbye and hugged each other even though Rosa would only be a few miles away.

Once again, Eddie and Rosa got into Mr. Jeter's Model T and rode the three miles to the house of Eddie's aunt who knew nothing about the wedding. Eddie and Rosa got out of the car. Rosa said goodbye to her father and followed Eddie into the house.

Eddie said, "Aunt Nora, I want you to meet my wife."

Miss Nora stopped dead in her tracks and looked at Eddie in amazement, then she said, "Did you say your wife?"

"Yes, Ma'am, we were married today in town."

"You mind to tell me that you bring some gal in here without telling me; do you know whose house this is? Not yours."

Rosa was beginning to feel very unwelcome. Tears were welling up in her eyes and started to run down her face.

Eddie said, "I am sorry, Aunt Nora. I should have told you. I hope it is alright. It is a fine time to ask if it's alright. You are here now."

"Where are you two going to sleep? Did you think about that? Lord, I don't know what's wrong with young folks these days. They don't think before they jump."

Rosa turned and walked toward the door, tears still falling from her face.

As she walked away, she heard Aunt Nora say, "Where do you think you are going, child?"

Rosa was still holding the clothes that she had brought with her.

"Put your bag down until we can make some arrangements. The only place we have right now is up in the attic."

The house was built with part uncut logs and partly cut lumber. The attic was made of mostly logs; there was enough space up there for a person to stand up straight in some parts. There was an old iron bed up there with steel springs. They put some old blankets on it to make it soft to sleep on. It was not much, but at least, they had a place to sleep. The old steel springs made a lot of noise with the slightest movement.

Rosa and Eddie had been living with his aunt for about two weeks. Rosa helped with the house cleaning and other work that went with country living, like looking after the chickens and hogs and milking the cows. Eddie was busy looking for work, but there was a depression in the land. There were no jobs anywhere. Most of the country was out of work. Times were hard.

Eddie came home late one evening from being out looking for work with no success; there were no jobs to be found. He climbed the ladder to their little space in the attic. Eddie, tired from walking all day, fell across the bed.

Those steel springs started singing a tone, then Rosa was glad to see him and sat down hard beside him; those springs sang some more.

Aunt Nora's voice ranged out below, "What are you, chaps, doing up there? You have no manners at all. You ought to be ashamed of yourself, acting like animals."

Eddie called down from the attic, "Aunt Nora, we are just sitting on the bed."

Aunt Nora said, "You are lying. You have no manners at all."

Rosa's feelings was hurt. She was being blamed for something that didn't happen. The following day, Rosa packed her bags and went home crying all the way; her feelings had been crushed. She felt that she could not put up with staying in Miss Nora's house any longer.

*****

That Sunday—about sundown, just as it had played out many times before—a lone figure of a man came walking through the footpath puffing on a Lucky Strike cigarette. Only this time, he was not happy, and he was not whistling. He was turning over in his mind what he could say to Rosa to make her feel better and come back home.

When Eddie approached the house, everyone was sitting on the porch drinking Kool-Aid made from fresh spring water. Mostly, they were waiting for the *Amos and Andy* show to begin on the radio.

Eddie walked up to the porch and greeted the family. Mrs. Alice said Rosa was inside. Eddie walked inside and greeted the sisters. Rosa got up and walked through the kitchen to the back porch and sat on the steps. Eddie sat down beside her.

After sitting there without speaking for what seemed like a long time, Rosa broke the silence. "I can't live in the house with your aunt. We need a place of our own."

"Where?" Eddie asked.

"No one is staying in that house over there," Rosa replied.

Eddie said, "There is one thing we are forgetting: I don't have any money, and there are no jobs to be found. President Hoover got everything all messed up. They tell me that there are no jobs anywhere."

"Maybe Mr. Thursday will let us stay in that house over there until you can find a job."

Eddie replied, "I don't know, but I'll ask him."

Eddie asked Mr. Jeter to introduce him to Mr. Thursday. He wanted to ask him about renting the house across the field. The house was not much, but it was better than what they have now. Mr. Thursday is the landowner that Mr. Jeter is sharecropping for. Three or four other farmers are also sharecropping for Mr. Thursday.

The next day, Mr. Jeter and Eddie headed to Mr. Thursday's house. The house was a large white building with many rooms. There was a pasture that came up almost to the back of the house. The pasture was home to many mules, horses, and other farm animals.

Mr. Jeter knocked on the back door. The maid came to the door. Mr. Jeter asked to see Mr. Thursday.

Mr. Thursday came to the door and said, "Can I help you?"

Mr. Jeter said, "This is my new son-in-law, and he was wondering if he could stay in the house behind us. The problem is he doesn't have a job. He was wondering if he could move into the house, and when he finds a job, he will pay the back rent."

Mr. Thursday looked at Eddie up and down for a few seconds, then he said, "That house is for sharecroppers. If you need a job and a place to stay, sharecropping it is. Do you know anything about farming?"

"No, sir," Eddie answered, "but I can learn."

Mr. Jeter said, "I would help him."

Mr. Thursday said, "Alright, it is done. David, you show him the ropes. Cut out five or six archers over there around the house. Let him have Julia, she is a relatively easy mule to work with. If you want to make anything this year, you better hurry."

Then Mr. Thursday turned to David and said to take him down to Mr. Man's store and help him set up an account so he can buy some stuff to start his family.

Eddie didn't want to be a farmer, especially not a sharecropper, but with the country in a depression, he had no other choice if he wanted a roof over his family's head; the only thing he could do right now was to try his hand at sharecropping.

Rosa was now in her eight months of pregnancy; the new family had settled in their house. There was not much to the house; mostly, it was only a shack. It had no running water, no bathroom, and there were wooden shutters for windows. But this was normal for most Black people of the time. They had to carry their drinking water a long distance. The building was not much, but it had a roof. It also had a fireplace for heat and a small kitchen for cooking.

*****

On April 3, 1946, Rosa went into labor. Her sister Annabelle was with her.

Rosa said, "Annabelle, go get Mama. I think the baby is coming."

Annabelle ran the short distance to their parent's house.

It took her a minute or two to get her breath then she said, "Ma, the baby was coming."

Alice yelled in the direction of the hog pin where David was looking after one of the hogs.

She said, "David, go get Miss Sue Pearl. Tell her to hurry, the baby is coming."

Miss Sue Pearl was the local midwife. Being excited about having his first grandson, David dropped what he was doing. He jumped into his Model T Ford and took off to get Miss Sue Pearl. The local midwife, Miss Sue Pearl, lived only a short distance away, and David made the short trip in a hurry. Miss Sue came to the door and asked if the baby was coming.

David said, "Yes, we need to hurry."

Miss Sue replied, "Let me get my bag. I will be right with you."

Miss Sue put on her white dress, a light blue apron, and white bonnet tied under her chin and her midwife bag on her arm.

She looked at David and said, "I am ready, but don't drive too fast. That baby is going to take its own time."

Annabelle had made a fire in the cooking stove and was heating some water in case Miss Sue needed some. Then out of nowhere, Rosa let out an ear-splitting yell that appeared to shake the room.

Miss Sue Pearl said, "Now look here, child—you stop that noise. You were not doing all that when you were getting this baby. You wanted to be a woman. Now you have it, so stop that noise and push. Stop it!"

It was a saying in the community that Miss Sue always tried to make her patients angry to help them manage their pain. A few more pushes and out came the baby.

Then Miss Sue said, "You see how easy that was, there was nothing to it."

Rosa rolled her eye at Miss Sue and said, "That's easy for you to say, you had the easy part."

Miss Sue cut the umbilical cord, tied it off, and gave the baby to Alice for her to clean up while she worked on Rosa. After Rose was taken care of, Alice put the baby in Rosa's arms. Looking at the baby, Rose was all smiles.

Then Miss Sue said, "I needed a name for the record."

Very quickly Rosa said, "His name is Eddie Gaston Jr."

Eddie's face lit up, and his eye began to shine when he learned that he had a son named after him.

Eddie worked hard at farming now that he had a family to feed and clothe. Mr. Jeter and Rosa's brothers helped him. It was hard work, but Eddie tried to make a go of it. He planted a small plot of peanuts to munch on.

In Cold Winter Nights

Finally, the cotton was ready to pick; the family worked hard to harvest their cotton crop. After the cotton was gathered and sent to the cotton gin, it was time to pay off and receive the reward for their hard labor.

It was the end of the cotton-growing season, and all the share-croppers were gathered at Mr. Thursday's back door to receive their share of the harvest. Eddie was very excited about finally having some money in his pocket. He had planned in his head what he would do with his share of the money. He planned to get little Eddie a new pair of shoes. He wanted to get his wife a new dress and buy some decent food for a change. He was getting more than tired of fatback gravy, biscuits, and pinto beans. He thought that he would borrow some-one's car and take Rosa and little Eddie to the picture show.

The screen door opened, and Mr. Thursday stepped out on the steps and thanked all the sharecroppers for this year's work. Then he called one of the sharecroppers.

"John, you did fair this year. I am sure you will do better next year. Your share comes to $1,000. James, $1,200. I think you will do better next year, you are learning fast. Bob, you did well this year at $1,500. David Jeter, you are the top man again this year. Your share comes to $2,000. Good job, David."

Eddie was the last one to be called. He could hardly wait to get his money. Eddie figured that he ought to get at least a $1,000. Little Eddie needed some shoes, and he wanted to buy Rosa something nice, and it would be nice to have some store-bought cigars for a change...

"Eddie Gaston..."

When Eddie heard his name, his heart began to beat a little faster. Finally, he would have some money in his pocket.

Mr. Friday said, "Eddie, you did not crack even this year. Maybe next year, you will do a little better."

Eddie's eyes were getting bigger and bigger until they looked like two moons shining in a dark sky; others said that his eyes looked like they were about to pop out of his head. Eddie leaped for Mr. Thursday, but Mr. Thursday was too fast; he ran into the house and locked the door behind him. Eddie tried to get into the house, but Mr. Jeter stopped him and convinced him to leave the ground.

Late that evening, the police came and took Eddie to jail and charged him with assault with the intent to do bodily harm.

Somehow, Mr. Jeter got Eddie released from jail. For Eddie, that was the end of sharecropping; he would need to find another way to support his family, but the family managed somehow. The incident, at the payoff, gave Eddie two nicknames: one was Pop because his eyes looked like they were about to pop out of his head; the other was Shine and Moon Shine because it was said that his eyes shined like two moons in a dark sky. Those names stuck with Eddie for the rest of his life.

*****

The year was 1953, the Gaston family was still living in Mr. Thursday's place but in a different house; now, they were renting, not sharecropping. The house was worse than the one they were sharecropping out of, but they had a roof over their heads; it leaked when it rained, but you could call it a roof.

Eddie finally got a job at the Palmetto Quires in Columbia, South Carolina, where they made concrete building blocks. Eddie and other men in lower Fairfield County traveled the twenty miles to work each day in the work bed of an old Ford pickup truck.

Working on the quarry was hard work, but it was better than sharecropping.

Learning to Write His Name

fter about a year of working at the quarry, Eddie became the subject of the joke of the day, which made him very uncomfortable and somewhat embarrassed.

Every Friday, around four o'clock, it was payday at the quarry; the men would gather around in front of the office to receive their paychecks. Eddie was the only one in the group who could not read or write. To receive their checks, the men had to sign the paybook. The men would make fun of Eddie because he had to make an X to receive his check. Eddie would wait to be the last to pick up his pay because he did not want anyone to see him make his X on the paper. When everyone had received their checks but Eddie, the jokes would start.

Someone would say, "Okay, Eddie, your turn."

Eddie got up very slowly.

Someone would say, "Now Eddie don't makes that X too big because you don't have much paper left."

All the men would laugh.

Then someone else would say, "Somebody, give him a good pencil, he might break that one. Make sure you make that X nice and pure now."

Eddie was too embarrassed to say anything. He forced a slight smile and kept on walking; he was smiling on the outside, but on the inside, his heart was full of shame. Even though the men laid on the jokes a little heavy, Eddie took it all with a false smile, but on the inside, he was very hurt, and the shame was almost too much to bear. Eddie was determined that he would have the last laugh. He knew how he would do it: he would learn how to write his name.

*****

Eddie and Rosa had four children by now: Eddie Junior, the oldest, Willie James, who died as an infant, Jessie James David, and Rosa Lee.

Almost every day, Eddie would bring a newspaper from work. Sometimes, the paper would be two days old. After the kids had gone to bed at night, little Eddie could hear his mother reading the article to their dad. One story that stood out in Eddie Junior's mind, even to this day, was the story about a young Black boy who was launched because it was said that he whistled at a White woman. There were stories about prisoners breaking out of jail and being on the loose.

But one night, Rosa was ready to read the paper. Eddie SENIOr lowered his head and spoke in a very serious tone of voice and with his head down, looking at the floor, not looking at his wife as he spoke to her.

He said, "Rosa, let us not read the paper tonight."

Rosa noticed the change in his voice; she had never seen this level of sadness in his voice before.

Rosa, beginning to get a little worried, asked, "What's wrong with you, Eddie? What's wrong? Are you sick?"

Eddie looked up at her and said, "Oh no, nothing like that."

Well, taking a lot of time to say what he did not want to say, he said, "Rosa, I want you to do something for me."

Rosa began to be very concerned and a little worried. Eddie had always been the happy-go-lucky type. Rosa had never seen this level of seriousness in him before. Eddie was a person who never let anything worry him.

Eddie looked up at his wife again then looked down at the floor, and said, "I want you to do something for me."

With a higher level of concern in her voice, Rosa asked what it was.

Eddie, still looking at the floor, said in a voice that sounded like a little child, "Rosa, I want you to teach me to write my name."

Rosa looked at him for what seemed like a long time, then she turned her head, got up, and said, "I need a glass of water."

Then she went into the kitchen; when her back was turned, she began to wipe the falling tears from her eyes, but the more she wiped, the more the tears fell. Rosa cried for so long until Eddie called her and asked if she was alright.

Trying to hide the trembling in her voice, she said, "I am okay."

After a few minutes, Rosa pulled herself together and walked back into the room.

Eddie looked at her and asked, "Are you sure you are alright?"

"I am fine," Rosa said with a very assuring voice. "After all these years, why do you want to learn to write your name now?"

Eddie told her the story of the men making jokes about him every payday because he has to make an X.

Again, fighting back the tears, Rosa said, "I'll get some paper. Eddie Junior ought to have some in his bookbag." Rosa found some paper and pencil and began to teach Eddie to write his name.

Eddie Junior was in bed, but he was not asleep. He could hear his mother giving his dad his first lesson. They started with how to spell his name. Then they went to the ABCs, which Eddie learned very quickly. The three days he went to school must have helped. By this time, Rosa and Eddie had three children. Eddie Junior, Jessie, and David. Before the teaching started, they all had to be in bed.

Eddie Junior was listening to the teaching. Rosa sounded off a letter, and Eddie Senior would repeat it. They did that over and over until Eddie Senior could replicate it on his own.

After a few minutes, Rosa said, "Now let me hear you spell your name on your own."

Eddie Senior took a deep breath and started to sound out the letters E-D-D-I-E G-A-D-S-O-N.

"Very good," said Rosa.

Rosa had Eddie Senior repeat the spelling repeatedly until *Eddie* Senior could do it with one breath without any mistakes.

After about an hour of practicing, Rosa said, "That would be enough for tonight. Tomorrow night, we will start making the letters with a pencil."

Eddie Senior and his wife, Rosa, climbed into bed, blew out the old oil lamp, and went to sleep. Although, Eddie Senior could not sleep very well for thinking of writing his name at last. He was thinking that soon, he would not have to make the X.

Eddie Senior didn't sleep very well that night. He had his mind on the day that he would be able to write his name on that paybook as pretty as you pleased and no longer would he be at the busy end of a bad joke. For about a week or so, Eddie and Rosa were busy practicing writing. Rosa turned out to be a good teacher; however, she only had a sixth-grade education, which was as far as the neighbor school would go for Black children. When they finished the sixth grade, they were expected to go to work in the White man's cotton field picking cotton.

*****

It was a Monday morning. Eddie Senior was standing by the side of the road waiting for his ride to work. He had to make those twenty miles riding in the work bed of an old pickup truck with a canvas top to keep out the rain and wind. Friday was five days away, and payday was when he would show off his writing skills. This week, he would spend all his practice time on writing in courtesy. They made it to work on time with a few minutes to spare. Eddie Senior was in a good mood today as he greeted other workers in passing. They noticed that he acted like he had a secret that no one knew about but him. The men would walk past him and see that he had a half-smile on his face just about all day. Eddie Senior was working smiling and whistling a tone; occasionally, he would start to sing one of those songs he learned singing in the Pine Grove church choir.

Eddie used all of his free time practicing his writing skills; Wednesday to Friday, Eddie was sharpening his writing skills. This was Eddie's big day. Eddie Senior even took an extra set of clothes so he could change out of his work clothes and look good when he made his name-writing debut. All the men were standing waiting to get their paychecks. Eddie walked up.

Someone said, "Here comes Pop, all dressed up to make his X."

Eddie kept walking until he was at the head of the line. He wanted his name to be the first one on the paper so that everyone after him would see it.

All the bosses were standing around drinking from some paper cups, waiting to collect their paychecks. The foreman of the concrete block part of the company looked up and saw Eddie at the head of the line waiting with a half-smile on his face as if he was hiding some deep dark secret.

The foreman asked Eddie, "What in the world are you doing at the head of the line? You are usually the last one to get your check. What are you doing all dressed up like you got a date? If you do, I will tell your wife."

They both laughed, and the foreman walked away.

The paymaster walked out of the office with a box of checks under his arm.

He looked at Eddie and said, "Eddie, this is the first time you have been at the head of the line. Are you in a hurry?" The paymaster looked through the significant stake of checks until he found Eddie's paycheck. "Alright, Eddie, come on, make your mark on that top line right there," he said, pointing to the spot.

Eddie took the pencil in his right hand, shrugged his shoulders just a little, put the pencil to his mouth, and licked the tip, then he put all that practice to work and wrote Eddie Gaston as if he had been doing it all his life; he took the check and walked off with a bit of bounce and swagger in his walk.

As he walked off smiling from ear to ear, a voice rang out, "Hey, Pop, I thought you could not write."

"Well, I didn't feel like doing it before. Making an X is so much easier. But I will tell you what I will write from now on."

All eyes were on Eddie. He was having the time of his life. But Earnest was not at all happy. He was the lead jokester when it came to Eddie; now, he felt like the joke was on him. He was planning how he could get back.

*****

All gathered in the back of the 1954 Ford truck and headed up Highway 215 home. Everyone was happy that a hard day's work was over, but Eddie was more than glad; he was excited. He was delighted because it was payday, and he was happy because he had pulled off the joke of the year. There were no more jokes about Eddie and his X from that day on. Eddie signed his name just as surely as he please every payday. But Earnest was not done with this; he smelled a rat somewhere: something just didn't smell right.

Eddie and Rosa have now been separated for two years. Not getting any support from her husband, times were hard for the Gaston family. Rosa got a job working at a poultry plant. The plant was hard work, but Rosa did the best she could to feed her family and keep clothes on their backs and shoes on their feet. The extended family members were hard on Eddie Junior for staying in school and not staying home to help his mother. All wanted Eddie Junior to stop school and help his mother. Many in the extended family were always reminding Eddie Junior that he needed to stay home and help his mother. By this time, Rosa had gotten a new job working at a laundry mat. Every day, on her lunch break, Rosa would wash dry and press Eddie's school clothes for the next school day; it seemed like everyone wanted Eddie to stop school but his mother.

Eddie was not thinking about stopping even though every teenager for miles around the countryside had stopped school or had never started. He could still hear in his mind the sound of his mother teaching his father how to write his name. Eddie would never forget the sound of a grown man being taught to write his name. Most of Rosa's brothers-in-law were hard on Eddie because he would not stop school. Every time someone mentioned stopping school, Eddie could hear the voice of his teachers saying, "Young man, stay in school. If you are going to make it in this world, you will need some learning."

At the age of twelve, Eddie Junior got a job at the local chicken farm. Eddie's job was feeding the chicken and gathering the eggs. Eddie and another boy named John took care of and gathered the eggs from six thousand chickens each day. The other boy's name was John. John had already dropped out of school even before he had learned to read, write, or count.

It was time for the evening egg gathering. They gathered the eggs in baskets that were made with iron wires; each basket had five rings of wire that held together many vertical wires which held the basket together.

It was important to count every egg at each gathering and keep a record of how many eggs each house was producing. If a house was not producing enough eggs to pay for their feed and turn a proof for the owner, that house would be sold for food.

One day, as Eddie and John were gathering eggs, Eddie noticed that some baskets appeared to have more than sixty eggs in them.

Eddie said, "John, are you counting the eggs?"

John held his head down and very softly said, "I can't count."

Eddie didn't tell John that he was not counting the eggs himself, but the years of gathering eggs had taught Eddie that the third ring up from the bottom of the basket was where about sixty eggs would be.

Eddie looked at John and said, "Don't worry about it, what I do is fill the basket up to the third ring from the top which will be about sixty eggs. By that time, the boss who was the owner's son also observed that some of the baskets appeared to have more eggs than the sixty.

Eddie answered but hesitated and said, "John said he could not count, but we worked out a system that would help come up with the right amount in each basket."

With a slightly angry tone to his voice, he said, "Tell me your system so I will know."

The boss pointed to a basket and asked Eddie how many eggs were in that basket.

Eddie looked at the basket and said, "About sixty-five."

The owner said, "Okay, let us count them and see."

After the count, there were sixty-five eggs in the basket.

After counting four baskets, he said, "Okay, from now on, fill the basket up to the third ring."

Eddie looked at John. He did not look happy at all; he did not say a word to Eddie the rest of the day. He was very upset because Eddie had told the boss he could not count.

Well, things were not very well between John and Eddie. The summer out-of-school days were ending; it was about time for Eddie to go back to school. John was still upset because Eddie told the boss that he could not count.

Eddie and John were in the boss's 1955 dark green Ford pickup truck. John was in the back, and Eddie was in the front with the boss's son who was driving.

They rolled up to the rear of the boss's large brick house.

The driver parked the truck and turned off the engine, then he reached into the back seat, picked up a newspaper, pointed to a section of the paper, gave the paper to Eddie, and said, "Read this."

Eddie read what he told him to read.

The boss's son took the paper from Eddie, folded it up, and said, "You can read now, so you don't need to go back to school anymore. You just come here and go to work."

Eddie did not say a word. He looked back at John who was grinning from ear to ear. But Eddie never said a word.

There were only a few days left before school started back. John and Eddie were in one of the larger chicken houses putting chicken feed in the feeder's bend. They heard a voice coming from outside of the front door.

The voice yelled, "Hey, John."

John answered, "Yes, sir."

The voice said, "Come here a minute. I want to talk to you."

John stopped what he was doing, making his way carefully through the hundreds of chickens and went outside; after some small talk about what a good worker John is, the boss got around to asking John what he wanted: which is to find out if Eddie was quitting school and going to work full time.

He said, "John, tell me something, did Eddie say he was stopping school and working full time?"

"He didn't say," John replied.

Then he put his hand on John's shoulder in a fatherly kind of way and said, "John, I want you to do something for me. I want you to find out if Eddie is going to school or not and let me know. I know I can depend on you, okay?" Patting John on the shoulder, the boss got into his car and drove off.

John did not say anything to Eddie right away. After about twenty minutes or so, John made his move. Eddie was taking a break from carrying the heavy sacks of chicken feed around. John came over to where Eddie was sitting. John sat down near him with that ready-made grin that John wore contently which was broader than ever today.

With an unusual tone to his voice, John said, "Eddie, are you going to go back to school this year, or are you going to stay here and work?"

Eddie looked John in the eye and said, "Look, man, I am not quitting school to spend the rest of my life in some stinking chicken pen. If he wanted someone to quit school to take care of some stinking chicken, let him make those grandboys, Jim and Dan, quit school and do it. That will be a good job for them."

Jim and Dan were the boss's small grandchildren whom he loved dearly; it appeared that the old man loved those grandchildren more than he loved life itself. When he was around his grandsons, he was a different person.

John could not get to his feet fast enough to get to the boss and tell him what Eddie said.

John found the boss outside picking up pecans that had fallen from the large pecan tree just outside the chicken house's front door.

As he approached the boss, the boss said to John, "What did Eddie say?"

John was more than happy to tell what Eddie said and more; this was his chance to get back at Eddie for telling the boss that he could not count.

As John approached the boss, the boss was the first one to speak. "Well, John, what did Eddie say?"

John was very happy to tell what Eddie said and more. That grin on John's face had gotten wider.

While still gathering pecan, the boss said, "Well, what did Eddie say?"

John began to speak. "Well, Eddie said if you want someone to quit school and work in some stinking chicken houses, you should get those two no-good grandboys of yours to quit school and do it."

This made the boss angrier than John had ever seen him before. Walking at a fast pace with chicken flying everywhere getting out of his way, he made his way to the feed room where Eddie was. His face was almost covered with red blood veins popped out all over his face like a thousand bloody rivers showing against his white face; he pushed open the door very hard and headed right straight for Eddie and slapped him hard across the face, then he grabbed a stick broom and attempted to hit Eddie with it, but Eddie was not having that. Eddie was not going to let that man hit him with that broomstick. Eddie grabbed the broom, and the tussle was on; there was more action in that seed room than ever before. Eddie would not let go of the broomstick, and the man could not take it from him. Upside the wall knocking down feed sacks, Eddie was still holding on, knocking holes in the wall. Eddie was still holding on to the stick.

All the time, the boss was yelling, "Let go of this stick."

But Eddie held on for dear life. Eddie was determined not to let that man hit him with the stick. It was only a few minutes, but it seemed like hours to Eddie. The boss let go of the broom and stepped back. His face showed less anger and more concern about what Eddie was going to do next. Eddie threw down the broom into the corner and walked out.

Eddie heard the angry voice ring out, "Where are you going? Get in here and feed these chickens."

Eddie kept walking and did not stop until he was at home. Eddie did not tell his mother what had happened. He kept it to himself. His mother sensed that something was wrong.

She asked, "What is wrong Eddie Junior? You are not yourself today. And why are you home so early?"

Eddie replied, "I just didn't feel good, so I came home early."

Eddie didn't want his mother to know that he was fighting with a White man in Fairfield County.

In the Land of the KKK

Eddie found out later that it was the KKK he was tussling with. Eddie stayed home from work for about two weeks. One day, the boss's son came to Eddie's home riding on a farm tractor, mainly because where Eddie and his family lived, the road was all washed out from the summer rain. A tractor was the only vehicle that could get to the house. He drove the tractor to the front door of the house. Eddie was standing in the doorway.

The boss's son shut the engine off so that he would not have to talk over the loud motor and said, "Eddie, I need you to come back to work. All that has happened is forgotten."

Eddie did not feel good about working for the man again, but they needed someone to work, and Eddie needed a job. To the chicken houses, they went; Eddie felt that something just was not right. But his mother needed some help taking care of and feeding the family, and Eddie felt that he needed to do his part.

On the way back to the job, Eddie was sitting on the old Ford tractor finder; the road was so bumpy that Eddie thought he would fall off at any mount, but he was holding on for dear life; they made it to the main road. They drove the short distance to one of the large houses. Right away, Eddie was put to work gathering eggs into metal baskets. John was also in the same house gathering eggs. When John saw Eddie coming toward him with an egg basket in his hand, the look on John's face showed for the first time that he was very happy to see Eddie. He learned that feeding and gathering eggs from six thousand chickens was hard work for one person alone. Even though John was happy to see Eddie, he still had a sore spot for him.

John was the first to speak. "Eddie, so you are back. I see, so you are not going back to school after all."

Eddie looked John in the eye and said, "John, let me tell you something, as soon as school starts back, I am out of here. I am here only because my mother cannot afford to buy clothes for me and my brothers and sisters to wear to school. If the truth be told, the man is using me to get the work done, and I am using him so that I will have something to wear back to school. I think I can put up with him for a little while longer.

The relationship between John and Eddie seemed to be improving, but still, Eddie did not trust him. Well, John and Eddie work hard together, and now and then, John asked Eddie if he is going back to school. Eddie's answer is always the same unwavering yes without any hesitation; yes, knowing all the time that John was only the messenger boy for the boss.

The boss's son decided that he would set a little trap for Eddie so that he would have no choice but to go to work or go to jail. The boss's son was a real character; he was a stone drunk. He was always on and off the wagon. He would stay sober for a month or two then something would happen and off he would go again.

One hot summer day, John and Eddie were taking a break outside one of the houses. John found a whiskey bottle that was about one-quarter full of a bright green liquid. John knew that the boss's son was a drunk, so John decided to give the bottle to him. The boss's son looked at the bottle and looked back at John and Eddie.

He put the bottle to his nose again; this time holding it there a little longer, then with a very serious look on his face, he turned first to Eddie and then to John and asked, "Did you two put something in this bottle?"

Eddie answered, "I didn't."

John answered, "I didn't."

The boss's son looked at both Eddie and John to see if he could see any sign that they were not telling the truth. He stood there with the bottle in his hand which began to tremble. Then his eye got cold-looking, and a very mean look came over his face; he had begun to perspire. His hand began to tremble. One at a time, he looked

John and Eddie in the eye. After looking at both of them for a few minutes each, he slowly raised his shirt and revealed a pearl handle 45 revolver.

He put his hand on the trigger and pointed it at each of them, one at a time, and said, "I am going to drink this. If either of you know any reason why I should not, you better speak now because if you put something in this bottle, this may be your last day on this earth." Then without another word, he raised the bottle to his nose and took a long smell then, with a quiet move, raised the bottle to his lips and poured the contents of the bottle in.

Then without looking at John or Eddie, he threw the empty bottle into the grass, put the 45 revolver back into his belt, and without looking or saying anything to John or Eddie, he turned and walked away. John and Eddie both collapsed on the grass.

Eddie Sets Up for Blackmail and Walks on the Water

Eddie was a good dependable worker. Even at a young age, Eddie was operating the egg grading machine, and he did not have to be told what to do. Eddie knew what was needed to be done and did it. But that was not the main reason they wanted Eddie to quit school. They did not want any Black boys in the neighborhood to finish school. So far, they had been successful. No Black boys for miles around had graduated from high school. One of the reasons was that if they could keep the Blacks uneducated, they would have a cheap workforce and keep them in what they call "their place."

All the chickens had been fed. The morning egg gathering was complete. Eddie and John had some downtime until the next egg gathering. But before sitting down to rest until the next egg-gathering time. The boss's son drove up in the dark green pickup.

He said, "Have you finished the feeding for today?"

John and Eddie said yes.

"That's good," he said. Then he got that very serious look on his face and said, "Eddie, I want you to take a little ride with me."

Eddie climbed into the front seat of the truck, and off they went to the boss's sister's house, about a half-mile away.

The boss's sister had a young daughter about fourteen years of age. Eddie remembered overhearing a conversation between the daughter and her mother, sometime before, about buying a horse. Eddie remembered that after some pleading with her mother, the young girl got her wish, only on one condition: she would be the sole caretaker of the house. She alone would have to take care of the house. They arrived at the boss sister's house in about eight minutes.

The boss's son went inside the house, and in about twenty minutes, he came back out, called Eddie out of the truck and said, "Eddie, I want you to go down to the horse stable and throw some hay down to the horse."

To Eddie, this seemed to be a strange request. Eddie was under the impression that it was the daughter's job to take care of the horse. Maybe she was not feeling well. In Eddie's mind, it made no difference whose job it was; they were paying him to work, so he went to the barn, climbed up into the hayloft, and began pushing hay down to the horse. Eddie was in the hayloft for about three minutes or less when the young girl who owned the horse came up; she did not say a word, just came up to Eddie, pushed him down on the hay, and fell on top of him. It was hard to stand up on all the loose hay without someone pushing on you.

Eddie pushed her off, jumped up, and said, "Don't do that."

He tried to be as calm as he could. She pushed Eddie down again and fell on top of him. Eddie started to remember his mother reading the newspaper to his dad about a young Black boy who was launched for whistling at a White woman. Eddie was wondering what they would do to him for lying in the hay with a very young White child about thirteen years old. Eddie kept pushing her off him trying his best not to hurt her. Then out of nowhere, there came a sharp voice coming from downstairs.

The young girl stopped what she was doing and said, "Yes, Mother."

"What are you doing up there?" yelled the mother. "Come down from there right now."

By this time, Eddie panicked and jumped out of the two-story window. Eddie hit the ground running.

It was all downhill, a very steep hill; at the bottom of the hill, there were two ponds with an earth dam between them. There was a footpath that led from the barn to the pond. The footpath led across the dam. To get across the dam, one would have to make a sharp turn to go across the dam. When Eddie hit the ground, he was moving at a speed that he had never reached before. He was running too fast to make the turn to go across the dam. When Eddie hit the water, one foot was in the mud, and one foot was in the water. Eddie was moving so fast that the foot that was in the water did not have time to go under the water. At the other end of the dam, Eddie stopped to catch his breath. After a few minutes, Eddie walked up the other side of the hill to the chicken house and started back to work feeding chickens.

After about an hour, the boss's son drove up in the green truck. He told John and Eddie to come go with him; he drove to the barn that Eddie had just jumped out of. The boss's son led John and Eddie to the side of the barn that Eddie had jumped out of earlier. He looked up at the window and then down at the ground under the window. Then he pointed to the footprint where Eddie had jumped out the window.

He said, "Here is where someone jumped out of this window. Look how long those steps are, he must have been moving."

John and Eddie followed him as he continued to follow the tracks.

As he was following the track, he pointed and said, "Man, he is moving now. Looks like he has picked up some more speed."

When they reached the pond, he stopped and said, "Now this is what I don't understand. I see where he went into the pond right here, and I can see where he came out of the water here, and it looks like he is still running. Do you suppose he can walk on water? I just don't understand it at all."

John was standing behind him with the largest grin Eddie had ever seen. John was enjoying this. To him, this was better than sweet potato pie.

The boss's son turned and walked back up the hill, got into the trunk, and headed to the chicken houses with Eddie and John sitting on the tailgate. The son's house was only a short distance away. On the way, they stopped by the son's house; the son got out of the truck and went inside, and after a few minutes, Eddie and John heard what sounded like arguing coming from the boss son's house. After a short while, the boss's son stepped out of the house and got into the truck with a .30-30 lever-action rifle in his hand. He climbed into the truck with the rifle and drove off, headed to the boss's house. He pulled up to the back of the strong-looking red brick house with a screened-in back porch and stopped the truck.

The boss's son got out of the truck, taking the .30-30 rifle with him. He walked to the back of the truck where John and Eddie were sitting.

He raised the rifle until it was pointing at Eddie's chest and said, "Do you think this will put a hole in you?"

Eddie was about to speak when they all heard a car coming with its motor racing to the breaking point; all three of them turned to see what car was making that noise and the motor running that high. They spotted the car—it was the car of the boss's son's wife; she only lived a few hundred yards from where Eddie, John, and the boss's son were. She was driving a jet-black 1957 two-door Chevy. It looked and sounded like she had her foot in the tank. All three of them including the boss's son were looking at the wife coming down the highway at a breakneck speed. The road to the boss's house where Eddie, John, and the boss's son were parked was an unpaved road with loose gravel on it when the boss's son's wife turned off the main highway onto the loose stone. Gravel, dust, and loose stone were flying everywhere. She put on the brakes, and the car slid about twenty feet before it came to a stop. The boss's son's wife was opening the door before the car came to a full stop. The car was still sliding as the boss's son's wife was opening the door to get out. In the meantime, the boss's son still had the .30-30 rifle pointed at Eddie with his finger still on the trigger. The wife rushed toward her husband, and with a single move, as if she was a pro, snatched the rifle from his hand in one move.

She said in a very angry tone, "What in the world do you think you are doing?"

Her husband replied, "I was going to kill me a nigger."

For the first time, the grin on John's face had turned to fear. The boss's son's wife took the rifle and told her husband to get in the car, and off they went. John and Eddie went to work in one of the chicken houses; they did not say a word to each other about what had happened.

The plan to force Eddie to quit school did not work; Eddie did not tell his mother anything about what happened.

*****

Eddie completed high school and obtained a job in Columbia South Carolina at the state mental health hospital as a medical-surgical aid; all new aid workers had to go to nursing school two hours a day and work on the hospital floor six hours a day practicing what they learned in class and applying what they learned in class,

In Eddie's class, there were three young White ladies, one White male, and two Black males. After studying a particular nursing treatment in class, the trainees would go to the hospital floor and practice what they learned in class. One of the White girls would always select Eddie to work and train with; this was the year 1964, and there was a wide gap between Black and White folks. Eddie knew that a young Black man spending too much time with a nice-looking young White woman could lead to trouble in the year 1964. She always selected Eddie to work and train with. Eddie knew that being in the state of South Carolina, a close relationship between a White female and a Black male would lead to trouble. He wanted to do something about it, but Eddie felt that if someone was nice and friendly to you, you should treat them the same. However, the training instructor did not see it that way.

One day, Eddie was called to the trainer's office. She was an older White lady who was the training nurse. Being from the deep South, she believed that White females and Black males should not be that close.

She said, "Eddie, I am going to have to let you go now."

Eddie did not have to ask her why because he knew why.

"Do you have anything to say?"

Eddie said, "Miss Lee, I was taught from a very young age to treat everyone nicely the way you want to be treated, especially if they are nice to you. I need this job. If you fire me, I will be nice. If you keep me, I will still treat people better than they treat me, but I need this job."

The nurse looked at Eddie and said, "Go on back to work."

She called the young White lady in and fired her.

One day, as Eddie was taking care of patients, the nurse in charge came to Eddie and said, "Eddie, I need you to go to the brown building. there is a young man there who needs an enema. I need you to give him one. On your way, stop by the supply office and pick up an enema kit."

Eddie was wondering why he had to leave the main hospital to give a patient an enema when the employee there had the same training he had. Eddie decided to do what he was told to do. But it was a strange request.

Eddie started on his way after stopping to pick up an enema kit. Eddie went to the brown building, still wondering why he needed to go there when everyone there had the same training and had been working longer than he had.

When Eddie walked into the building and saw his patient, all his questions were answered. There lying on the bed was a young Black man about twenty years old who was struggling for every breath; his eye had turned a bright yellow, and his stomach was knotty and as hard as a brick. Feces were protruding out of his rectum and had turned black. And he appeared to be fighting for his life. Eddie called the charge nurse; she came, and after examining the young man, she called the doctor who came to examine the young man and gave him an IV.

The doctor looked at Eddie and said, "Do the best you can."

Eddie completed what he was supposed to do. When the task was completed after about an hour, the young man took his last breath and died. He was about twenty-five years old. The aids and technicians that were supposed to be taking care of him were sitting in the office drinking coffee. They did not want to touch that boy just because he was Black; they just let him die. To them, it was just another nigger gone.

Eddie stepped in the office door and said, "I hope you all had a good cup of coffee while you sat here and let that young man die, but if someone went to jail, that won't happen again like that." Then Eddie turned and walked out on his way back to his job.

The head nurse looked at them as if she wanted to say something but she didn't.

She walked out with Eddie and said, "I know how you feel, Eddie, but you cannot change the whole world by yourself in one day.

Eddie said, "No, but somebody has to try. If no one ever says anything about gross neglect and poor nursing care like we just saw, we will get the same thing over and over again. Maybe I cannot change the world alone, but I can try, and if enough people try, they can move a mountain. But here, no one is trying. Most people would not let a dog die like that young man did. They would shoot him first."

The nurse and Eddie walked back to the main hospital. And Eddie heard no more about the treatment of the young man.

After Eddie had worked at the hospital for about two years, one day, Eddie was preparing to go to lunch; he made sure that all of his patients were taken care of and headed for the elevator, which would take him from the third floor to the first floor where the lunchroom was. Eddie waited patiently for the elevator door to open; finally, the door opened. On the inside, Eddie was surprised to see the boss of the chicken farm, his wife, his son's wife, and the boss's sister and her daughter. Eddie did not recognize them at first because they were not wearing farm clothing.

Eddie stepped into the elevator and said, "Hello, how is everybody today?"

No one said a word; they all looked at the wall. As if to say, it is better to look at the wall than this uppity nigger.

Eddie finished his lunch and came back after about an hour; as he was passing the nurse station, the nurse in charge said, "Eddie, come here a minute, will you?"

Eddie came closer, and the nurse leaned over and said in a whisper, "Do you know someone named Manning?"

Eddie said, "Yes, I worked for them at one time. Why did you ask?"

"Oh, no reason, and oh, Ms. Johnson wants to see you before you go back to work. She wants you to wait here for her."

After a few minutes, Mrs. Johnson, the head nurse, came over to the nurse station where Eddie was standing and said, "Eddie, I am going to transfer you to the fifth floor." She could look at Eddie's face and tell that he wanted no part of the fifth floor.

The fifth floor was where the TB patients were housed.

The man's family was trying to hide from Eddie that their son was in a mental institution. They were not worried about Eddie, but they didn't want the community to know where the son was. They were sure that Eddie would tell.

When Eddie learned that the boss's son was in the state mental hospital, his hand began to shake, and he had to go sit down for a while. Eddie was thinking that all this time, he was dealing with a crazy man. Two times, this crazy man had pointed a gun at him. The first time was when he told John and Eddie that he would shoot them with a 45 pistol if they had put anything in the whisky bottle. The next time was when he held a .30-30 rifle on Eddie and said he was going to kill him a nigger. Eddie's hands were still trembling as he made his way to the fifth floor.

Eddie also learned that this was not the first time the son was a patient in the mental institution. Eddie was told that every time the son was missing from the farm, he was in the state hospital. Eddie decided that he would keep the family secret only because he worked for the hospital.

Eddie Got Drafted
into the US Army

Eddie was drafted into the United States Army where he went to school to become a diesel mechanic. After completing diesel school, Eddie was shipped off to South Korea where he worked in the motor pool as a mechanic. After working as a mechanic for a few months, Eddie was assigned as the motor pool compound gate guard. Eddie and a Korean police officer guarded the gate afterhours. It was also Eddie's job to walk around the compound every so often checking it to make sure that all was well. There were also seven US soldiers who had sleeping quarters at the compound. The compound faced a busy Korean street in the city of Soul.

One evening, Eddie and the Korean officer sat in the gate shack observing people walking the street. As they were observing the walkers, they also noted that five of the soldiers who had sleeping quarters on the compound were coming toward the gate, and they all had a Korean female with them. Somehow Eddie was smelling trouble. So he told the Korean officer to take care of the gate until he got back. It was time for Eddie to check the compound for trouble. Eddie took a long black nightstick and started on his round checking the compound. Eddie was gone for an hour or a little more; when he returned, he found that the Korean officer had let the soldiers and the young Korean females into the compound. Three or four Korean police were also there. One of the young Korean females was accusing one of the soldiers of rape. Eddie went to the soldiers' living quarters to investigate what had happened. When Eddie entered the building, all seven of the soldiers appeared to be sleeping. There was female underwear on one of the beds. Eddie put what he saw in writing and gave it to his commanding officer. Eddie's report was published in the Korean newspaper the next morning. The soldier who was accused of rape was tried and put in jail.

*****

Eddie was discharged from the army and obtained a job as a mechanic at three different places and reclaimed his job at the state hospital part-time; until one day, he noticed an ad for employment at the Southern Railway in the state newspaper. Eddie decided to apply for the job but believed in his mind that he would have no chance of obtaining employment with a company like the Southern Railroad.

Eddie got dressed that morning. Following the newspaper's instructions, Eddie made his way to the site to apply. When he got there, he had a mind to turn around and go home. There were about sixty or seventy people jammed into one room. Thinking that he had no chance to gain employment with that many people applying, just when Eddie was about to leave, a young man put a test paper in his hand.

He said, "Try to answer all the questions. When you complete the test, return it to me."

Eddie completed the test in short order and returned it as instructed.

After some time had passed, the same young man came to the front of the room and said, "I want to thank everyone for coming today. On behalf of the Southern Railroad Co., we thank you. Will the flowing persons please remain? John Dearman and Eddie Gaston."

After all the others had left the room and the two of them were informed that they were the new employees of the Southern Railroad, Eddie was blown away to learn that out of sixty people in the room, he was one of the two that was hired.

Eddie showed up for work at the Railway office ready to go to work. The boss of the shop looked Eddie up and down giving Eddie a very disagreeable look.

Then he pointed with his chin and said, "Sit down over there."

Eddie took a seat in a chair nearby and waited for what seemed like hours.

Getting a little impatient, Eddie stood up and said, "Sir, I am here to go to work for the Southern Railroad."

The gentleman behind the desk replied with a very sharp tone of voice saying, "I know what you are here for, boy."

The man behind the desk was the boss of the railroad box car repair man.

He looked at Eddie and said, "Father, I don't believe he made the score I am looking at on this test. I am going to put you to work cleaning out box cars until we find out more about this. I think you're lucky for making this score."

Eddie did not mind the wait at all. He was happy to have a job with decent pay and good benefits.

Eddie worked hard cleaning out box cars; the work was hard, but the pay was not bad for cleaning box cars, and the benefits were good. Eddie was working with two older Black men in their sixties. Eddie had fun listening to them tell old railroad stories and trying to teach him the way of the Railroad. Eddie worked about a year cleaning out box cars; the young White man that was hired with Eddie had gone to the railroad school, completed it, and was back on the job repairing box cars and working as a railroad car repairman.

One day, Eddie was called to the office; when he arrived there, he met a White gentleman wearing a white shirt and brown pants. Eddie learned that he was the railroad test person. He was there to test Eddie again because the boss and others didn't believe that Eddie got that high score that was on the original test.

The man with the test sat Eddie at a small table and said, "I need you to take the test you took when you were hired one more time."

Eddie looked at the gentleman with a puzzled look on his face. "Why?" Eddie asked, but before the gentleman could answer, Eddie said, Okay, I will take the test again."

The test person gave Eddie the test and said, "Do the best you can, and when you are finished, bring the test to me. I am going to have a cup of coffee."

Before the tester could finish his second cup of coffee, Eddie had finished the test and was handing it to the tester.

The tester said, "You finished that mighty fast, would you like to look over it again before I check it?"

"Thank you, but I think I got it," Eddie replied.

The man giving the test took a sheet of paper from his briefcase and began checking Eddie's answers against the one he had on the paper.

After a few minutes, he looked up at Eddie and said, "You did well, the same grade you had before."

The boss looked at Eddie and said, "I don't believe it."

The boss told Eddie to go back to work. Eddie did as he was told. But all the time he was working, he was trying to figure out why they were so interested in his test score. Eddie just could not get it off his mind.

*****

It was Friday evening and Eddie's turn to have the weekend off. After the wife had cooked a good supper, Eddie ate a good helping of chicken and rice and two glasses of iced tea. Eddie grabbed the day's newspaper and began to look it over; by chance, he saw an ad from a cement plant for a diesel mechanic. For some reason, Eddie didn't know why he decided to apply for the job knowing all the time that he was not leaving the railroad. Eddie was working the evening shift at the railroad, so he had time to apply for the job before going to work at the railroad.

Eddie made his way to the cement plant about five or six miles away; when Eddie got there, he walked inside and greeted a man who appeared to be in his late thirties sitting at a metal desk eating what appeared to be a late breakfast with coffee.

Eddie greeted the gentleman who was not much older than he was; the gentleman returned the greeting and said, "Can I help you?"

"I would like to apply for the mechanic job that was advertised in the state paper," Eddie replied.

"Have you ever worked as a mechanic before?" asked the man at the desk.

"Yes," Eddie replied, I was a mechanic in the army."

"But do you know anything about diesel engines?"

"Yes," Eddie replied, I studied diesel work in the army."

"Alright," the man replied. He reached into the desk drawer and took out two sheets of paper; he handed Eddie the papers and said, "Answer the questions the best you can and return them to me."

Eddie began to read the questions on the paper and, almost midway, realized that it was the same test that he took for the railroad job.

Eddie finished the test in short order and gave it back to the foreman of the cement plant. The man looked at the paper and compared Eddie's answers to the answers on another sheet of paper. After checking all the answers, the man looked at Eddie with a strange look on his face; he looked at the paper a little longer before he dropped Eddie's paper in the trash can and looked at Eddie with a half-apology in his tone and said, "I am sorry, I can't hire you. If I hired you, you will have my job. Thank you for coming."

Eddie went back to the railroad with a more positive attitude. Eddie thought they hated him because he was Black. But what Eddie didn't know was that now they hated him because he was Black, and they thought that he was smart. They didn't want Eddie, a young Black man, to have the job that they thought they should have.

The Plot to Get Eddie Fired

Eddie was working the evening shift that week; he was working on the third track that ran parallel to the path that the first shift took to get to their cars and go home. Seven or eight men were getting off from work that evening, and all of them stopped right at the spot where Eddie was working. A tall slim fellow whose nickname was toes—they called him toes because his feet were so long that they appeared to get where he was going before his body did—left the group and started walking toward Eddie, then the whole group stopped and started looking in Eddie's direction.

When Eddie saw the entire group stop and began looking in his direction, Eddie guessed that something was going to take place, but he did not know what. Eddie decided to stay on his guard whatever happened.

When Toes got a little closer to Eddie, he yelled, "Hey, boy," so everyone in the shop could hear him.

Eddie looked up and looked around the shop as if he were looking for a boy.

Then Toes said, "I am talking about you, boy."

Six men were working in the shop that evening; all had stopped working to see what would happen between Toes and Eddie. Toes was an older White man in his late sixties and ready to retire. That probably was the reason they selected him to start something with Eddie, but Eddie was not falling for it. Eddie walked up to within five feet of Toes; by this time, everyone in the shop was looking at Eddie and Toes. Toes was in his late sixties but looked older; Eddie was in his early twenties.

Eddie looked at Toes, waited for a few seconds, and said, "You know something, Toes. Beside you, I guess I am a boy." Then Eddie turned and walked off.

Then everyone took a deep breath and started laughing.

Well, it appeared that Eddie won the battle between him and Toes. But Eddie had a deep inner feeling that the confrontations were not over. There was much more to come.

*****

A week had passed since the encounter between Eddie and Toes; Eddie had a strong feeling that there was much more to come. The campaign to get Eddie fired was just beginning; there was more to come.

Eddie was working the second shift on track number 1 with a young White man called Jim. Jim was in his middle thirties, and to Eddie's surprise, Jim was the one selected to get Eddie rallied up that night. For the first hour or two, things were going well between Eddie and Jim

Then out of the blue, Jim said, "Eddie, you know something?"

"What is that, Jim?" Eddie replied.

"I don't like Black people, none of them including you. All of you are lazy, and they are always looking for someone to give them something. Everyone knows that all Black people come from monkeys. Look at your long arm's nappy hair, big lips, and big noses."

"Well, Jim," Eddie said, "it looks like I need to educate you on why the parts of our bodies are different. Let us start with the hair— why is your hair straight and my hair is curly? Why is that? Well, let me start with myself. My hair is curly because my place of origin is Africa, and Africa has a very hot climate, therefore, my hair is curly so that air can blow through my hair and keep the brain cool. The brain is the control center of the body. Likewise, your hair is straight because your place of origin is a cold place, therefore, your brain needs to stay warm, so your hair is straight, and in layers, to keep the brain warm. Likewise, I come from a hot place, therefore, my nose is big so that I can take in enough air to keep my body at a safe temperature to keep it cool in the hot climate. My legs are long to run fast to get away from danger, whatever the danger is."

Jim said, "Well, I just don't like Black people, and I still don't like you."

Eddie said, "Jim, I will be careful how I say that if I were you."

"Why do you say that?"

"Well," Eddie replied, "I have never seen a White man with hair like yours. You ought to be proud because the only animal that has hair like yours and mine is a sheep, and they are almost human. They have a menstruation cycle like the human female."

Jim is a White man who has a head full of curly light brown hair. Jim looked at Eddie for what seemed like a long time, then he dropped the tool that he had in his hand, and up the hill, he went to the boss's office.

After about twenty minutes or so Jim came back; he walked straight to Eddie and said, "What about a shaggy dog?"

Eddie tried hard not to let him see him laugh; to make Jim feel a little better, Eddie said, "You are much better than a dog. It will have to be a high-class dog."

Eddie said, "There is nothing wrong with being a Black man. Being a Black man will put you in some high-class company. After all, Jesus was a Black man. The Bible said that his hair was like a lamb's wool, just like mine, and his feet like burned brass. That sounds very much like a Black man to me. If you don't believe me, touch on a piece of brass and see what happens. It will turn black."

Jim and Eddie went back to work and said very little to each other the rest of the night.

*****

The next work night, Eddie was working with a quiet fellow who did his work and did not have very much to say. We will call him Red. That night, Red and Eddie were working on shop track number 2. They had pulled in a box car with a bad shock absorber; the shock absorber was a very important part of the box car as well as other railroad cars. They help to assume the shock when two or more cars come together; they are made of steel and were very heavy. A shock absorber weighs about five to seven hundred pounds.

That night, Red and Eddie had to replace one of them. They used a cutting torch to cut bolts holding the absorber in place, then they used a jack that was made for that; after they got the gear down and, on the jack, Red started trying to secure the absorber. Red was studying lumbering with the jack. It looked like they spent about thirty minutes on that jack trying to get that gear in place. Eddie got impatient and asked Red to step aside. Eddie reached down with both arms and lifted that seven-hundred-pound piece of steel from the jack; right away, Eddie knew that he had made a wrong move.

That he was in trouble there; he stood with seven hundred pounds of steel in his arms and did not know how to put it down safely. If he dropped it, the large hunk of steel would crush his feet; it was too heavy to walk with. The only thing he could try was to swing it out over his feet and drop it. Eddie took a deep breath and with all his might, he pushed the seven hundred pounds hunk of steel away from his feet, and it worked. Eddie tried to act like nothing was wrong, but it felt like all the bones in his body were welded together.

Red went up the hill to the boss's office, stayed about thirty minutes, came back, walked up to Eddie, and said, "Eddie, I don't like you."

Eddie looked at Red and said, "That's alright, Red, but I like you. I can't help but love you because you are made in the image of God who made us all." Then Eddie looked Red in the eye and said, "I love you, brother."

Red looked at Eddie for what seemed like a long time.

Looking back at Red, Eddie noticed that tears began to well up in his eyes, and all at once, the tears began to fall. He was crying so hard that the water from his eyes appeared like two small waterfalls flowing down the side of a mountain wetting his bright blue shirt. Eddie stood there looking at a big heavy man who weighed about 240 pounds standing there crying like a baby who has lost its mother. Eddie began to feel sorry for Red. The tears in his eyes let

Eddie know that Red had a good heart. From that night on, Red was Eddie's friend. Eddie thought they were trying so hard to find a reason to fire him that they missed one right under their nose when Eddie lifted that five to seven-hundred-pound shock absolver which would be unsafe work practice.

The campaign to get Eddie fired appeared to have lost its traction until one night when Eddie was working the midnight shift. Eddie was on time for work, but he was the last one to arrive at work. The neighborhood was not so good where the railroad workspace was. Now and then, they would have someone's car or truck get broken into. Eddie drove up and parked in the last parking spot. Eddie and almost everyone else were driving pickup trucks. Eddie noticed that every truck had a shotgun over the back glass; some had their guns propped in a rack in the front seat. Eddie said to himself, "Now they know that this is a bad neighborhood. All those guns out in plain sight don't make sense."

There were about eight or ten trucks there that night, and it appeared that all of them had guns in plain view. Eddie started for the work area but stopped and went back to make sure his truck was unlocked; the work parking had break-ins as before.

After Eddie greeted everyone getting ready for work, Eddie said, "Well, fellows, I think we will have a break-in tonight. Everyone dismissed Eddie's comment as just talk.

Everyone worked hard that night and was happy that the night was over. Some were going home, and some were going hunting; some had new shotguns and were eager to try them out. But to their surprise, they found that Eddie was right: every truck had the windows broken out; others had the back glass busted out, and all of them were broken but Eddie's.

*****

The next work night, as the second shift was standing around the punch-in clock preparing for work, everyone was very quiet, no laughing and joking around. Eddie walked up and said good evening, but not a person said a word. They acted as if they didn't hear him.

The foreman of the evening shift walked up and said in a very demanding tone, "Eddie, the boss wants to see you in the office right now."

Eddie walked up the hill the short distance to the boss's office. He was sitting at his desk with a very angry look on his face.

Eddie spoke and said in a very polite tone, "Good evening."

The boss did not say a word, just kept doing what he was doing.

After a few minutes, he looked up at Eddie, then he said in a very angry tone, "I don't want to look up at you."

Eddie took a seat in the chair in front of the desk and waited for what seemed like a long time. After some time had passed, the boss said, "Eddie, I understand that you were responsible for the break-in last night, your boys broke in every truck out there but yours."

Eddie looked the boss in the eye and said, "What do you mean I am responsible for the break-in? You think I had something to do with it? What brought you to that conclusion?"

The boss said, "Will you explain to me why your truck was the only one that was not vandalized? Everyone else's truck was broken into but yours, everyone else had their stuff stolen but yours. Explain that to me?"

"Yes, I can explain it very well," Eddie replied. "First, I, just like everyone else here, know that we are in a bad area, and the young men in this area have no jobs and are just looking for something to steal so that they will be able to buy some of the things they want and need. But I cannot aford to donate to their cause. The reason why all *your* trucks and cars got broken into every other week is that you invite the thief to do it."

"What do you mean we invite the thief to do it?" replied the boss, looking at Eddie with a very angry and puzzled look, and saying, "It looks like you are the one doing the inviting. Your truck has never been vandalized, and I want to know why."

Eddie looked the boss right straight in the eye and said, "*I will be more than happy to tell you why*. My truck has never been vandalized because first of all, I am not stupid. I have sense enough not to put anything of value in plain sight for the thief to see and want to steal. Second, I never lock the doors of my truck because I don't want my winders broken out. What will happen if the thief will open the door and go through my truck? Not finding anything to steal, they will close the door back and go to the next truck with those fancy shotguns in them and have a ball. Father, I think that anyone who believes that a thin piece of glass will stop a thief is not thinking straight."

The boss looked at Eddie for a minute and said, "That makes a lot of sense."

From that day, everyone started leaving their truck doors unlocked and nothing in them to steal, and the vandalism stopped.

*****

Eddie had been feeling a strong call to the ministry, so he resigned from the railroad and went back to school to get his BA degree. Eddie worked at Belk's department store in Columbia, South Carolina, to take care of his family at the same time while trying to earn a degree to become an African Methodist Episcopal Church minister.

Eddie started working at Belk's Department Store as extra help during the Christmas shopping season. Eddie was working with a young very friendly White girl who had a physical deformity in one hip which caused her to walk with one hip higher than the other. She had a thin face and a head full of very partly golden-brown hair that reached halfway down her back. It was as if nature had taken all the beauty she had and put it into her hair.

The Christmas season was in full swing; people were buying gifts of all kinds. There was one item that was selling like hotcakes: the Madam Alexander doll. A middle-aged White lady came into the toy department wanting to buy a Madam Alexander doll; Eddie asked her if he could help her.

She replied, "Yes, I want to buy a doll, but I don't see one. Looks like they are all sold out."

"What kind of doll are you looking for?" Eddie asked.

"I am looking for a Madam Alexander. But you don't seem to have one."

"I will check the stockroom and see if there is any left," Eddie replied.

Eddie left his customer waiting on the floor and headed for the stockroom. Eddie pushed the stockroom door open and walked in, and to his surprise, he came face-to-face with his coworker Mary who was coming out as he was going into the stockroom. They almost bumped into each other; there were not six inches left between them.

Mary looked up at Eddie, and in a very soft whisper, said, "I am going to stream."

Eddie had been living in the deep south long enough to know what that meant.

Eddie turned around, went back to his waiting customer, and said, "There are no more dolls, but give me your phone number, and when we get some more, I will call you."

All the rest of that week, Mary and Eddie did not speak to each other; they communicated only when they had to as the job called for it. They made it through the holy days around the second week of January.

The manager came to Eddie and said, "Eddie, I want you to go downstairs and work in the young men's department."

Eddie was not pleased with the move because he liked working in toys, but after a very short time, he learned that he liked the young men's department better.

One day, as Eddie was in the corner of his department straightening up the clothing on the rack, a tall young White man, who appeared to be in his late twenties, made his way to where Eddie was working.

He said, "Do you know a girl named Mary? She has long brown hair down her back and is a kinder foxie."

Eddie answered and said, "Yes, I know her, we worked together for a whole—"

He looked Eddie in the eye and said, "That's my girlfriend."

Eddie tried to think of something nice to say, saying, "Wonderful, she is a nice girl."

The young man left the department and left Eddie wondering what that was all about. Eddie didn't know it at the time, but he was soon about to find out.

*****

About two or three days later, two new people came to the store: a Black girl in her twenties and a young Black man about the same age. The Black girl went upstairs to work with Mary, the young man went downstairs to work with Eddie; unknown to Eddie and Mary, the young man and the young woman were police officers who were hired to investigate the claim made by Mary that Eddie was harassing her.

After the two officers had been there about two days, Mary came walking through the department where the new helper and Eddie were working.

The young man who was working with Eddie asked Eddie, "Have you been messing with that?" referring to Mary.

Eddie replied with a simple no. But he was wondering why he would ask him a question like that, not knowing that this was a police officer asking the question. Eddie bushed it off as men talked and left it at that; there were other questions and comments that Eddie wondered about. All the questions were in some way about Mary. Eddie brushed it off as just a young man interested in females. Eddie had a friend who was a contractor and repaired houses for a living. Eddie drove a red long-bed pickup truck to work every day, and the friend asked Eddie if he could borrow his truck to haul some lumber for a job he was working on.

Eddie said, "Okay, but I will need the truck back tomorrow when it is time for me to go to work."

The day went by fast; the friend told Eddie that he would pick him up when the time came.

"No, I know where you are. I will walk over and relax on the park benches until you are finished."

The friend said, "Okay, have it your way."

Eddie hang up the phone and went to sleep.

*****

The next evening, Eddie was on his way to get his truck; when he got there, the truck was still loaded with lumber. Eddie had lots of time, so he made his way to one of the tables in the park and waited. As he sat there, two young men walked up; one sat on one side of Eddie and the other one sat on the other side.

One of them said, "You are here just taking it easy."

Eddie said, "No, I am waiting for my truck to get unloaded so I can go to work."

By that time, five or six police cars had gathered down the street.

Eddie said, "I wonder what all those police cars are doing down there."

One of the young men sitting at the table with Eddie said, "They must be looking for someone."

Eddie looked down the street and said, "They must want them badly to have that many cars."

Eddie had no idea that the police were there for him.

As Eddie and the two undercover police were sitting there making small talk, suddenly, they heard a car traveling at a high speed in what appeared to be second gear. The car was coming in Eddie's direction. The car was a small Ford straight shift; from the way it sounded, it appeared that the car was in the second gear, and the driver had the window down. Eddie could recognize the driver.

Eddie said, "What is she doing over here and driving like a fool with all those police cars down there? What is she doing over here anyway?"

One of the undercover officers asked, "Have you been messing with that?"

"No, we worked at the same place, that is it."

With that, the two young men got up from the table and walked in the direction of the police cars.

Eddie got into his truck and headed for work; he got there with time to spare. Eddie went to his department and began straightening up things that were out of place. He noticed a police captain coming in his direction. They had talked about a week before, but Eddie did not know that he was being investigated; as he got closer, Eddie realized that the police officer and he had talked before.

As he got within speaking range, he said, "How are things going, Eddie?"

Eddie said, "Things are going well, thank God." Then he asked, "How are you?"

He replied, "I am doing alright for an old man. Are you still in the seminary?"

Eddie replied, "Yes, I have about four more months to go, then I will be finished, thank God."

"Where are you going then?"

"Wherever the church sends me."

The captain replied, "You know I forgot that you were in the AME Church."

"That's right," Eddie replied. When the church sends me, I go.

Then the captain got a more serious look on his face. He said, "Eddie, do you know a young lady named Mary Ann?"

Eddie replied, "Yes, I worked with her at one time upstairs."

"Well, Eddie, I want you to listen to me very carefully. If you see that young lady coming, walking down the street, you cross over to the other side. She is dangerous. She has been making complaints about you. But don't worry about it, and don't be all that concerned. We know that all she has been saying is not true."

"What has she been saying?" Eddie asked.

The officer said, "You don't need to know. We know it is not true, so leave it at that."

Then Eddie began to realize something: his telephone at home had to be tapped—that is the only way the police would know where he would be and when. Then Eddie began to realize that this thing with Mary was more serious than Eddie thought. When he saw her passing, he was afraid to say good morning, So he kept walking.

*****

Eddie completed his studies at the Lutheran Seminary and earned a master's degree. Eddie pastored several churches in South Carolina and was appointed presiding elder of the Manning district with the supervision and oversight of twenty-six churches and pastors.

About the Author

Eddie Gaston Jr. was born on April 3, 1946, in Fairfield County, South Carolina. His parents were Eddie and Rosa Mae Gaston. He is the oldest child of thirteen children. He graduated from Allen University with a bachelor's degree in social work with a minor in psychology and has a master's in divinity from the Lutheran Theological Southern Seminary.